ACROSS THE
ROMAN
WALL

THERESA BRESLIN

A & C Black • London

This edition 2005
First published 1997 in hardback by
A & C Black Publishers Ltd
37 Soho Square, London, W1D 3QZ

www.acblack.com

Text copyright © 1997 Theresa Breslin

The right of Theresa Breslin to be identified as the
author of this work has been asserted by her in accordance
with the Copyrights, Designs and Patents Act 1988.

ISBN 0-7136-7456-3

A CIP catalogue for this book is available from the British Library.

A&C Black uses paper produced with elemental chlorine-free
pulp, harvested from managed sustained forests.

Printed and bound in Great Britain by Bookmarque Ltd, Croydon

ROMAN WALL

Contents

1

Collision!

'Take care!' Marinetta's elderly house slave stepped in front of her young mistress as she spoke.

Dust rose further along the road from the potter's workshop where Marinetta had paused to look at a large urn on display in the open shop front. There was a noise of horses being driven at speed, and the people before her broke apart and ran towards the edge of the street.

'Out of the way!'

The crack of a whip stung in the air as the young charioteer, face dark with impatience, drove through the crowd.

'What is it?' asked Marinetta. 'What is wrong?'

'Stay back,' Lavinia urged her, 'else you will be knocked over.'

But Marinetta was not to be told. She loved her weekly shopping trips with the house slave, wandering along the Great Way which ran through the town of Corstopitum, stopping to look at the wares which the traders had set out. There was always something new and unusual to attract your eye, goods brought from all over the empire. Fine glass, strange cloth with deep dyes and rich patterns, wine in barrels, amphorae containing herbs, oils and sauces. And occasionally in the street, as now, something interesting would happen. A legion marching past on its way to the fort at Cilurnum on the frontier at Hadrian's Wall, or a juggler, some acrobats, or even one of the official postmen with letters from Rome itself.

'What is it?' Marinetta asked again. And she ducked under Lavinia's protective arm to get closer.

The young charioteer was coming down the road at a furious pace. He would surely kill someone, thought Marinetta, and she stepped back quickly, stumbling as she did so. As the hard rim of the wheels struck on the cobblestones a few yards away, Marinetta reached out desperately to steady herself and her fingers caught the top of a large urn outside the potter's shop. As she fell, she pulled it down with her, and it rolled out into the road.

The two black horses leading the chariot reared and pawed frantically, eyes rolling in fear. A curse escaped from the boy's mouth. He grasped the reins with both hands and managed to bring the horses under control.

'By all the gods!' he swore again, and glared about him. Then he and an older companion stepped down from the chariot. Speaking in common Latin, the boy addressed Lavinia.

'Who has done this to me? Delayed a messenger of the mighty Roman Empire.'

'You have done this to yourself,' the old lady replied calmly. 'He who makes most foolish haste, arrives last.'

'A slave should not be so insolent,' said the young man. 'Rudeness in one so old indicates lack of beating by the master of the house.'

Marinetta scrambled to her feet. How dare this boy speak to her slave this way! 'We are taught to revere our elders,' she addressed him. 'Disrespect to the aged is usually regarded as a sign of great stupidity.'

The young man walked forward and gave the upstart girl who had spoken to him a haughty look. He realised at once that she was a wealthy, upper-class young woman by her hair decorations, and by her dress, which was fastened with an ornate broach of dark gold set with gemstones.

He turned and spoke quietly in pure Latin to his companion. 'Britons are *so* provincial,' he said.

'And Roman officers are *so* arrogant,' replied Marinetta at once, also in pure Latin.

The boy stepped back in astonishment. The older man laughed out loud.

'Well said, daughter!' he cried.

'You speak very grandly for someone of little stature,' said the boy angrily.

'And you appear to have such a great

opinion of yourself,' said Marinetta. 'It is surprising that so small a chariot can accommodate such a large head.'

The older man stood a pace away from them, folded his arms and surveyed them both. 'Come now, Lucius,' he said, as the boy hesitated. 'My favourite nephew, it is your turn!'

'It would serve you well to have a mind of who I am,' the boy told Marinetta. 'I am Lucius Calvus, nephew of Titus Calvus, senior officer in the government of Imperial Rome, conqueror of all, centre of civilisation. You have detained me on important business for our emperor Honorius.'

Marinetta made a small bow. 'All hail Lucius Calvus,' she said. She beckoned to Lavinia. 'Come, Lavinia, let us proceed on our way and not keep Lucius Calvus any later from meeting with his friends to play dice.' Marinetta took her slave's arm and, lifting her skirts clear of the road, she began to walk away.

The older man clapped his hands. 'I think she wins, Lucius. I think she wins!'

'What an unruly girl,' said Lucius to his uncle as they climbed back into the chariot. 'I hope our paths never cross again.'

His uncle laughed and slapped him on the back, then tossed some coins to the potter who was sweeping up the remains of the broken jar. Lucius shook out the reins of his horses, but before moving off he turned his head to look at the retreating figure of the young girl.

'What an awful young man,' Marinetta told Lavinia as they continued down the street. She glanced back as she heard the chariot wheels begin to turn. 'I wish I may never speak with him again.'

2
Marinetta

Marinetta took Lavinia's arm and leaned on it a little as they walked on down the road. Her ankle ached from the fall, but she did not want to return home yet. She still had some provisions to buy for the evening meal. Her father had told her that he was expecting important guests. And although, since the death of Marinetta's mother some years ago, it was usually Lavinia who supervised most of the cooking and preparation of the family meals, Marinetta always selected the menus and liked to make little dainties for special occasions.

'Ave! Marinetta!' a voice from a side street called out. 'The girl with the golden hair!'

Marinetta stopped at the sound of her

name. At the entrance to an alley there stood a small stall with a faded striped awning.

'Salmanes!' cried Lavinia. 'I hope you have some treats for us. It is so long since we have seen you.'

'Here is some special nectar for my beautiful women,' replied the dark-bearded trader. He picked up a spatula and, scooping some thick amber liquid from a pot, he offered it to Marinetta. 'The bees have laboured long to match the colour of your hair,' he told her. 'But poor creatures, they have not been able to capture that honey hue.'

Marinetta laughed. 'We want some preserves, dried fruit and nuts,' she told him. 'I wish to make a cake this afternoon.'

'It is getting difficult to obtain certain kinds of goods,' he told them as they chatted. 'I came from Eastern Gaul last month and the hills are full of brigands. They say that some of the German tribes, the Goths and the Vandals, are gathering on the edge of the Empire.'

'I too have heard talk,' agreed Lavinia. 'There are barbarians everywhere.' She glanced around. 'They say there might be attacks...'

'Impossible!' declared Marinetta. 'The army is always here to protect us.'

'Yes...' said Lavinia slowly.

Salmanes frowned and stroked his beard. His face had a troubled expression. 'Now, before winter comes, I intend to make my way home while I can still do so safely. If the Roman legions do not control the roads, then travel will become too dangerous.'

'But no one could withstand the might of Rome,' said Marinetta. 'The Empire cannot fall.' She regarded Lavinia anxiously. 'Can it?'

Lavinia looked at Salmanes. Then she smiled at Marinetta. 'Rome is the centre of civilisation, conqueror of all,' she said. 'And we have it on the very best of authority, don't we? Lucius Calvus himself told us this.' She winked at the stall owner. 'A friend of Marinetta's,' she explained. 'We met him some moments ago on the Great Way.'

Marinetta's face went pink. 'That arrogant young man!' she exclaimed. 'I want nothing whatsoever to do with him!'

'Of course not,' said Lavinia soothingly. She addressed Salmanes. 'One can tell this is true by how loudly she protests.'

The stall owner smiled a broad smile.

'Nonetheless,' Lavinia went on. 'This Lucius, who is no friend of yours, is quite probably correct. Rome must be invincible.'

'There!' said Marinetta. 'Don't be anxious, Salmanes. All will be well.'

Across her head, Salmanes exchanged a glance with Lavinia. Then he shrugged his shoulders. 'Let us hope you are right, little one,' he said.

'Where did you hear this talk of attacks?' Marinetta asked Lavinia later. They had returned to her father's villa some miles from the town and were now busy in the kitchen.

'Oh, here and there,' said Lavinia. 'One shouldn't really listen to rumour and gossip. Yet...' She hesitated.

Marinetta looked at the old lady closely. Lavinia had been the house slave for many years and Marinetta knew her to be wise and full of good counsel. Marinetta's father, who was the local magistrate, often discussed politics and confided in her. It was not like her to be alarmed by tales.

'Yet?' prompted Marinetta.

'They say that there have been delays in the wages coming from Rome for the soldiers ... that some of the tribes north of here, in Caledonia, are arming themselves. There have been one or two incidents.'

'Does my father know of this?' asked Marinetta.

'Yes,' replied Lavinia. 'His guest tonight is a senior Roman statesman. They are to discuss the news which he has heard recently. Your father is deeply worried, and has been thinking of moving our household closer to the town.'

But my father is on friendly terms with the local tribes,' said Marinetta. 'My own mother was of the Votadini. We receive their emissaries with respect.'

'Not every tribe agrees to yield to Roman law,' said Lavinia. 'We have had raiding parties from beyond the Wall before, though not for many years,' she added.

17

Marinetta shivered. She looked to the kitchen door which stood open. It was late afternoon and already getting dark. Lavinia followed her gaze. She smiled gently.

'I shall light the lamps if you wish to gather in your herb basket and close the door,' she said.

Marinetta stepped outside. She did not think of the Romans as an occupying force. It was nearly four hundred years since Julius Caesar had first landed his invasion fleet on the southern shores of Britain. The troops stationed at Hadrian's Wall hardly ever went on manoeuvres, many had married local people. The army itself was now made up of different races who had all become part of the local community, bringing their own customs, beliefs and traditional ways. Many of the plants in Marinetta's garden were not of British origin, she knew. Some, like the cucumber, had been brought to Britain by the Romans. Their architecture had been copied everywhere, arches and columns and long straight roads.

Her father's villa was based on the Roman style, with interior designs of frescoes and mosaics. She would hate to leave this comfortable house with the hot water which ran in pipes beneath the floors, especially now, as winter approached. She looked across her gardens. The afternoon sun stretched long shadows on the grass. Marinetta gazed towards the trees. Beyond them lay the tracks which led to the frontier. She looked again and blinked. Were there other shadows there? Ones that moved among the dark greenery, silently merging with the mossy bark? She smiled at herself. She was remembering the spirits in the ancient Celtic stories her mother had told her. She picked up her basket and then stopped once more. She had felt for a moment as though eyes were watching her. Was there something in the bushes?

Suddenly a woodcock flapped into the air from the branches of an oak. Marinetta squealed in fright and then laughed out loud at her own silliness. She went in and closed the door of the kitchen firmly behind her.

Outside in the gathering gloom, shadows slipped among the trees, moving quietly closer to the house.

3

Garrison Headquarters

There was still a scowl on Lucius's face as he pulled his horses to a standstill and dismounted in front of the garrison headquarters in Corstopitum.

'Ho now, Vesta,' he said, patting the flank of the first black mare. She swung her head towards him, and he blew gently into her nostrils. With long slow movements he stroked her forehead. His uncle Titus smiled as he watched him.

'Are you more calm now, my headstrong nephew?' he asked.

Lucius glanced up. 'At times they annoy me so much, these Britons,' he said. 'They should be grateful that we brought them civilisation. I have read the accounts of our historian Tacitus. In the early years, when the legions first came here, most of the natives lived in round wooden huts. The smoke from their fire went directly through the roof! Can you imagine? They should appreciate the benefits of the Roman way of life.'

'Do you truly believe that those we conquer should show gratefulness,' asked Titus, 'and would you respect them if they did?'

'That is not the point,' protested Lucius. 'Look around you! There are aqueducts, latrines and bath houses. Who built these? The Romans. By all accounts, in the past, British sanitation was disgusting! How could they live without sewers to dispose of their waste, without fountains to supply clean water?'

'You don't miss what you've never had,' said Titus gently. 'Try to remember, Lucius, that not all of these things were Roman inventions. We adopted the best practices of the countries which we invaded. Being adaptable is why we have survived so long.' The older man frowned and then said half to himself, 'Let us hope we can continue to do so.' He smiled at Lucius. 'Come, let us see why Cornelius the garrison commander wishes to speak with me.'

'Alms, kind sirs. Alms, I beseech you.' A beggar blocked their path.

'Stand aside,' Lucius ordered. When the old man did not move, he brushed past him with an impatient gesture. 'Don't pester your betters,' he said as he walked on.

'Lucius!' his uncle reproached him. He shook his head at his nephew, and then paused to drop a coin in the old man's cup.

'The lack of proper news from Rome is worrying me,' Cornelius told them. 'I have written to tell our commander-in-chief of trouble brewing beyond the Wall, in Caledonia. But my letters have not been answered. I am sure they have not reached him. The painted ones, the Picts, are becoming bold again. Rumour is that the Scots across the water in Hibernia might attack, and in the south, there is always the threat of the Saxons from the sea. Yet there is no word of reinforcements...' His voice trailed off wearily.

'What news have you of our troop movements abroad?' asked Titus.

'Confused reports from various sources. There is trouble all over the Empire. Commander Stilicho has chased Alaric in Thessaly and Greece but still has to bring him to battle. We need more trained soldiers here.' Cornelius hesitated before going on. 'I have heard that some of our own men think it best to have another emperor...'

'Never!' exclaimed Lucius.

His uncle smiled. 'It has happened before, and not so long ago either.'

Lucius and his uncle studied the map which was spread out on a large table. It showed each milecastle and fort on the great Wall of Hadrian that straddled the land. On the northern parts of the map were written the names of the various tribes occupying those lands. 'Do you have details of any particular tribal movements?' asked Titus.

'This is difficult to obtain,' said Cornelius. 'Since we had to disband the areani—'

'The *areani*?' queried Lucius.

Cornelius glanced at Titus, who nodded.

'It was our spy network,' the garrison commander explained to Lucius. 'People who moved among the tribes in the wild areas and brought us information. But many of them became corrupt and sold details of our military movements to the barbarians. We no longer use them. I feel sure my own mail is being intercepted...' He raised his hands and dropped them. 'So I must take what steps I can... Which is why I have asked you to come and see me today.'

He addressed Lucius's uncle. 'There is a local magistrate, Cedric, who is a good man, and has expressed concerns for the wellbeing of his household. He has connections with the tribes of the Votadini and the Selgovae and has been trying to discover where the source of the trouble lies. Someone needs to speak to him and find out what he knows. I have arranged for you to dine privately with him this evening.'

'Do you think that an attack is imminent?' Lucius asked his uncle later.

'I don't know,' Titus replied. 'I have yet to

read the news which my own informant delivered to me earlier.'

Lucius stared at him. 'Your informant?' he repeated. 'I've been with you all day. Who was this person?'

Titus selected a bright red apple from the fruit bowl on the low table in the room. He took a little sharp knife from his belt and carefully began to peel it.

'Look now, Lucius,' he said quietly, as he carefully removed the skin. 'Here is an apple, with fiery red skin on the outer layer, and ... what is now revealed?' He showed his nephew the pale white fruit pulp which lay just underneath. 'A lesson for life,' he went on. 'Don't judge a man by the clothes he wears.' Placing his hand inside his tunic, he drew out a small, wafer-thin piece of curled tree bark with inked writing on it. 'The beggar slipped it to me. The old man whom a young boy pushed aside earlier was an emissary of Rome.'

Lucius's face flushed.

'And now,' Titus laughed, 'your skin is like the apple's.'

'I am sorry,' said Lucius at once. 'Uncle,

forgive my stupidity and ill manners.'

'I do,' replied his uncle. He passed the letter across the table to Lucius. 'What do you make of that?' he asked. Lucius examined the lines of tiny script for a moment or two. 'It's in code,' he said at last. 'Do you have the key?'

'A very simple one,' said Titus. 'A variation on Julius Caesar's own.' He took out a scroll from a cabinet and showed Lucius a poem. 'I have matched each letter of the alphabet with one of Catullus's poems. Unless you know this verse the message is impossible to decipher.'

Lucius's uncle studied the message, and then rolled it carefully into a tube shape. Lifting the hem of his cloak he undid a stitch in the seam with his knife and, placing the tube in the opening, he slid it along inside. 'This is grave news,' he said.

'What does it say?' asked Lucius.

For a long moment his uncle did not reply. Then he spoke slowly. 'You are old enough not to have the truth hidden from you. I am afraid that the forces of darkness are gathering all over the Empire, and may yet beat upon the gates of Rome. There is danger from tribal attack, and also enemies within. As Cornelius had suspected there are traitors here, along the Wall. This message tells me who they are. And they have at least one friend in Rome, a senator who plots against the Emperor. Tomorrow I myself will journey to Rome and make my report to Flavius Stilicho, commander-in-chief of the army.'

'Let me go with you,' said Lucius.

'No,' said his uncle, 'it is too dangerous. There will be those who will try to prevent these tidings reaching the ears of the Emperor Honorius.'

'I am not afraid,' declared Lucius. 'I will go and proudly proclaim the word of Rome.'

'Which is exactly why you would be so unsuitable a messenger,' laughed Titus. 'I am still uncertain whether to take you with me to dinner tonight. You speak far too readily when silence is required.'

'I will be silent tonight,' said Lucius. 'Please allow me to accompany you.'

'You will bear in mind then that this is an

important family we visit? You must be polite.'

'I will be unfailingly polite,' said Lucius.

'Even if you are provoked?' his uncle asked. 'You promise me that you won't lose your temper?'

'I foresee no problem,' said Lucius. 'I promise.'

4

Attack!

'I hope they have central heating in their house,' said Lucius as he and Titus rode out that evening. 'The weather on this island is always cold.'

'Hush,' his uncle scolded him.

As they reached their destination, a large spacious house set among flower and herb gardens, they saw a white-haired figure waiting to greet them.

'Welcome to our guests,' said the tall man as they dismounted. 'I am Cedric, master of this house and magistrate of these lands.'

'I thank you for your welcome,' said Titus. 'I have come from the garrison as arranged, with my nephew Lucius. We are honoured by your invitation.'

'Hail, in the name of the Emperor,' said Lucius formally.

The older man regarded the boy with a smile. 'I wish you good evening,' he replied. 'We are honoured that you dine with us.'

'What pleasant gardens,' said Titus. 'The flowers are well tended in your care.'

Cedric laughed. 'Not my care,' he replied, 'but my daughter's. Since my wife died, she is mistress of this house.'

'She must have skills in gardening. These herbs are difficult to cultivate,' replied Titus.

'Ah, here comes my daughter now,' said Cedric, as a young girl with long, golden hair came from the house.

Lucius turned round, and looked straight into the eyes of the girl he had almost run over in his chariot earlier in the day.

'Lucius Calvus!' exclaimed Marinetta.

Her father laughed in surprise. 'I did not know you were friends already,' he said.

'Friends!' repeated Lucius. 'I—'

He felt his uncle press his elbow, and murmur in his ear, 'Remember your promise, Lucius.'

Lucius closed his mouth quickly.

'I wish you good evening,' said Titus to Marinetta, 'and would like to compliment you on your most attractive house and scented gardens, which are only surpassed by your own beauty and sweetness.' He turned to Lucius with a wicked grin. 'My nephew is in complete agreement with me. Isn't that so, Lucius?'

Lucius swallowed and nodded once or twice. 'Indeed,' he managed to croak.

Marinetta looked at Lucius suspiciously. 'Indeed?' she said.

'Ah,' interrupted Titus quickly, as a faint chime sounded from the house. 'Would that be a signal that dinner is ready? Forgive my rudeness,' he went on, 'but I am ravenous and wish to sample some of these vegetables which you have grown.' He chatted on as they all went inside, and were led to their couches to recline as they ate, in the Roman fashion.

Marinetta was opposite Lucius, and could not help noticing that he ate four of her little seed cakes. She would take great delight in letting him know later that it was she who had baked them. Let him say then that Britons were provincial!

After dinner the two older men began to talk more seriously.

'I understand,' said Marinetta's father, 'that there are difficulties with law and order in many parts of the Empire.'

'News from the frontiers is unclear,' said Lucius's uncle carefully.

'That all depends,' said Cedric, 'on which news you receive. I have my own private sources.' He gave Titus a long look. 'As no doubt you have yours. I will speak plainly. My wife was of the Votadini tribe from beyond the great Wall of Hadrian. Many travellers pass this way and tell me of great unrest everywhere. Also, it is said that some of those who guard the Wall itself will allow raiding parties to come and go if the booty is shared.'

Titus Calvus remembered the words of the garrison commander. *This man can be trusted...* He sighed. 'Magistrate, you are right. There are uprisings in the Eastern Empire, and here in the Western Empire we have our own dangers. This afternoon I was brought the names of disloyal army officers based in Britain. They are linked to a senator in Rome who favours his own candidate as Emperor. I carry this message with me and I believe that our commander-in-chief Stilicho should be made aware of what it says.' He lifted the hem of his cloak and showed them its hiding place.

Cedric spoke. 'We have enjoyed peace here for so long that invasion seems unlikely, but nevertheless I think I should move my household into the town. It is obvious that things are not as they should be. There are delays with the food supplies for the army, and it may be that the soldiers at the fort on the Wall will withdraw?'

'The Roman Army,' declared Lucius, 'is all powerful and will fight to the end.'

'The Roman Army,' replied Cedric, 'like any other army, will fight as long as it is paid.'

Lucius gasped. 'Such treachery!'

Titus shook his head. 'No, Lucius, Cedric has spoken wisely. Unfortunately it is a fact. If the men do not receive their wages, they might desert.'

'You share my worries then?' asked Cedric.

'Yes,' said Titus. 'Tomorrow I will brief Cornelius the garrison commander and then travel to Rome to ensure that Stilicho himself hears these tidings.'

'Let us share a glass of wine in peace this evening,' said Marinetta. She refilled their goblets.

In the kitchen, Lavinia gathered scraps for the dogs. Then she went to the door to call them in. She frowned as she rattled the bowl with her spoon. The two hounds normally came at a run. What was amiss with them tonight?

Lavinia walked to the end of the path and towards the outhouses, then stopped. There was smoke pouring out from the doors of the stables. As she stared in shock, red flames suddenly broke through the roof. Beyond the line of the trees, figures were moving, not one or two, but half a dozen or more; men with burning brands in their hands, men with swords and spears. Lavinia clutched at her heart. It was a raid! The tribesmen had come, as her master had warned they would. She gathered up her gown and hurried back to the house, shouting the alarm as she went, 'Alarm! Fire! Fire! Alarm! We are under attack! Fire!'

5

Captured

The sound of running feet and Lavinia's voice calling 'Fire!' made Marinetta jump up from her couch at once. Her father went to the window and pulled aside the curtain. 'The stables are on fire!' he shouted. 'Quickly, fetch water from the well!'

'My horse!' cried Lucius. 'Vesta!'

They ran from the house as Lavinia came in. 'Don't go outside!' she cried, too late to stop them.

Lucius raced towards the stables where they could hear the frantic whinnying of the horses. Marinetta ran with him. Thick smoke stung their eyes and made them cough. They both stumbled inside and opened the stall doors for the panicking horses. Lucius tried to catch Vesta's tether and calm her, but both animals galloped out of the door immediately.

'Look!' said Marinetta.

The stable boy lay on the floor. Together they dragged him outside.

'I think he is dead,' said Lucius. He knelt down and touched the boy's head. Then he looked at his hand. It was red with blood. 'This is no accidental fire. Someone has done this deliberately.'

Lucius looked up at the sound of hooves. Through the smoke came men on horses. He stood up and pulled Marinetta by the hand. 'Attack!' he yelled as he saw his uncle coming towards him carrying buckets of water. 'Behind you! Watch out!'

Titus dropped the buckets and turned round. The first horseman was almost on top of him. Reaching up, he pulled on the rein as the rider swept past. The rider raised his arm and felled him to the ground.

Marinetta was roughly hauled up by the next rider and carried away.

Lucius ran to help his uncle who had managed to half sit up. 'I can't stand,' he gasped. 'I turned on my leg as I fell.'

Lucius ducked as another horseman came close, whirling a sword over his head.

'We are outnumbered,' said Titus. 'Run, boy, run!'

'No, never,' replied Lucius.

His uncle groaned and slid back on to the ground. Cedric ran towards them. 'It has happened,' he said. 'As I predicted!' He looked around him wildly. 'Where is Marinetta?'

'There!' shouted Lucius. Marinetta was struggling with the rider who had carried her off. She was fighting furiously, kicking and scratching at his face. The horse reared as its rider lost control, and Marinetta fell on to the grass.

'You fight well,' said Lucius as he helped her to her feet.

But the fight was soon over. They were heavily outnumbered by the raiding party. Some men encircled them, while others looted the house. Lavinia was chased outside. Both she and Marinetta turned their heads away as burning brands were tossed into their beloved home.

The leader of the raiding party rode up to inspect them. He wore plaid trousers laced from knee to ankle, and a deerskin tunic. His hair was braided in two long plaits, which hung down his back.

'Leave the old man and the woman,' he ordered. 'Take the others.'

'My daughter!' Cedric cried. He held out his arms as Marinetta was dragged away. 'Marinetta... My daughter!'

Marinetta, Lucius and Titus's hands were tied. They were slung across the horses, and the group set off to the north east, loaded down with stolen treasures, gold, silverware and arms.

After travelling for an hour or so, they stopped when it was completely dark. Lucius strained to see what was happening. They had been following the line of the great ditch on the south side of the Wall for the last mile or so. He realised that they were now at one of the Vallum crossings. He saw two men slip away from the party towards the crossing gateway there. Perhaps he could alert the sentries? If he kicked his leg against the flank of his pony, would the noise the animal might make carry over such a distance?

As if sensing his thoughts, one of the other tribesmen moved nearer to him. He pulled a grimy knife from the belt at his waist. 'This knife slits throats if you make a sound,' he hissed

'I am not afraid to die,' said Lucius proudly.

The man looked at him. Then he grasped Marinetta roughly by the hair and pulled her head back. 'Her throat,' he said craftily. 'Any noise and I slit *her* throat.'

Lucius gritted his teeth and lay still.

After about a quarter of an hour the two tribesmen returned, and the horses were led forward through the now-open gate, under the archway and on to the Military Way. As they turned west on the marching road, Lucius felt sick to his stomach, for he knew that murder had been done. Then he saw the outline of a milecastle on the Wall just ahead. 'Ha!' he thought. 'Now they shall see the might of Rome, when they try to cross the great Wall of Hadrian.'

Again the party stopped, and the two

tribesmen went forward, but this time not so quietly. They seemed to be expected, as the gate opened at once. Lucius felt then as though he had been struck a physical blow. He was close to weeping as he saw Roman soldiers usher the enemy into the courtyard, and through the impregnable frontier Wall of the Empire. There was a tower above the second archway of the milecastle, but no sentry challenged them as they filed underneath.

'Treachery! Bribery and treachery!' The words choked in Lucius's throat.

They were now on the narrow pathway of the Berm, on the north side of the Wall. The prisoners and booty were lifted off the horses, and then the soldiers led the horses back through the gate. Lucius, Marinetta and Titus were roughly pushed from the narrow path down into the forward defence ditch. There were tribesmen waiting there, and also on the glacis slope facing them. Tribesmen with fast ponies. In a very little time they were moving swiftly north into the wild territories of Caledonia.

Many miles later, at the edge of a wood,

they made camp for the night. The prisoners were dumped in a heap on the ground, hands still tied together. The rogues must feel secure, thought Lucius, as he watched them light their fire. The men no longer spoke in low tones, but he could not make any sense of what they were saying. He whispered to Marinetta to ask her if she knew. The surly one with the knife kicked him.

'Quiet,' he snarled. 'You speak. You die.' He threw some food at their feet.

'The child shivers. She is cold, give her my cloak,' said Titus.

'Let her shiver.'

'As you wish,' Titus shrugged. He folded his cloak and tucked it under his head. 'She will be of less value to you suffering from a chill.'

The man leaned down and, pulling the cloak roughly away, he threw it towards Marinetta.

'Cover Marinetta with my cloak, nephew,' Lucius's uncle told him.

Lucius kept his eyes downcast as he carefully wrapped Marinetta in his uncle's cloak. Although his eyes did not meet his uncle's, he knew his intention. They had to retrieve the message from the cloak. When the raiders reached their tribal home they would share out the goods. A fine woollen cloak would be a prized possession. The coded message was sure to be found, and they would all be slaughtered as spies.

'Get away from her!' The tribesman kicked Lucius again.

Lucius rolled over on the earth and then sat up slowly. He glanced at Marinetta. Her complexion was pale, but she had a set expression on her face, as if she were determined not to show weakness. He dared not speak to her, not even in a whisper.

Would she understand why his uncle wanted her to have his cloak? Would Marinetta remember about the secret message and where it was hidden?

6

Trek North

By first light they were on the move again, and as they went deeper into the wood Marinetta knew that it was now almost impossible for them to be trailed by any rescue party. She thought of her father and tried not to let the tears come.

They rode for many miles, until the trees thinned out. Suddenly, in front of them, was a great marshy swamp. In the middle of this were some crannogs, houses built on platforms. The ponies were left tied to the trees as the tribesmen and their prisoners walked across the rough wooden planks to the dwelling places.

'Look!' sneered one of the tribesmen as he pointed northwards to a hill on the horizon.

'There is the wall of Antonius Pius and your great Roman fort at Cibra. See what remains of it now? Ruins!' He opened a door in what looked like a pigsty and flung them inside.

'Ruffians!' said Lucius, as soon as they were alone. 'That's what they are. All of these Celts are thieves and barbarians living in foul dwellings.'

'Not so,' said Titus. 'These Celtic people have a language and a culture of their own. Remember your manners. Marinetta's mother was of this race.'

Lucius's face went red. 'I spoke without thinking,' he admitted.

'As you often do,' his uncle reminded him. 'If you had paid attention to your history lessons, then you would know that the great Julius Caesar himself spoke highly of them. Their bards are gifted musicians and storytellers.'

'But, Uncle,' protested Lucius, 'they are so undisciplined. Their fighting method has no order.'

Titus held up his hands which were tied together. '*We* are *their* captives, Lucius,'

45

he smiled.

'Because they don't fight fairly!' protested Lucius. 'They don't follow proper military procedure.'

His uncle laughed out loud. 'Why should they do battle as we do? They fight according to their own rules.'

'And they enjoy it,' said Marinetta. She remembered her mother telling her of the great Celtic warriors, heroes who were honoured. The stories of the wars, with brave and noble deeds, and then the feasting afterwards which went on for many days and nights.

'Ah yes,' said Titus. 'To many men war is a game. I wonder what throw of the dice will now decide our fate.'

Lucius started to reply, but fell quiet as the door of their prison opened and they were ordered outside. The silver dishes, ornaments and hangings taken from Marinetta's home had been divided up. An old man came and took the woollen cloak from around her shoulders. Marinetta saw Lucius and Titus look at her. She made a slight nod with her head, and touched the folds of her skirt. The secret message was now hidden in her dress.

There was some discussion among the tribesmen, and then two of them who had taken no booty prodded the captives towards the walkway.

'What's happening?' Lucius asked his uncle.

'I think we are their share from the raid. These two look like wandering renegades so we are more use to them than heavy goods.'

'For what?' asked Lucius.

Titus did not answer. His leg was now badly swollen and he dragged it clumsily. When they were almost at the spot where the horses were tethered, one of the men suddenly pulled Marinetta and Lucius to one side. The other leaped onto his horse, and raising his sword high above his head, gathered the reins and rode straight at Titus.

'No!' Marinetta screamed.

Marinetta's shout gave Titus a vital second, and he moved and avoided the blow. He stumbled but did not fall, and began to hobble painfully, with his hands still tied, towards the shelter of the trees.

Then Lucius struggled free, and bravely ran forward to put himself between the rider and his uncle. 'Run! Uncle, run!' he yelled. 'Run for Rome! Run for freedom!'

The tribesman, in a fury, knocked the boy to the ground. Lucius rolled over and scrambled to his feet just in time to see his uncle reach the first trees. The tribesman wheeled his horse around and cantered back to his friend.

'No matter,' Marinetta heard him say in dialect. 'The wolves will finish him off.'

Whatever purpose they wanted us for, thought Marinetta, Titus was clearly no good to them with his wounded leg. What could it be?

Again they rode on, until the harsh crying of gulls told them they must be near the sea. Soon after they came to cliffs, and descended a rocky path to a little inlet where they all dismounted. One of the riders shaded his eyes with his hand and looked out across the bay. His friend muttered a few words.

Lucius looked at Marinetta. 'What is going on?'

She shrugged. 'I don't know. They say the ship from Gaul is late, and there isn't much time before nightfall.'

The two men looked at their prisoners and then spoke to each other again in lower tones.

'What are they speaking of now?' asked Lucius.

'Us,' said Marinetta.

Lucius gripped her arm. 'What do they say?' he asked.

'They are deciding our fate.' Marinetta's face became pale.

'What is it?' Lucius demanded. 'What are they saying?'

Marinetta turned to him. Her eyes had grown wide and dark with fear. 'They have arranged to meet a pirate ship here. We are to be taken across the sea and sold as slaves.'

7

Sold into Slavery

'Sell us? How dare they! We are citizens of
Rome!' cried Lucius, jumping to his feet.

The two men turned and glared at Lucius.
Then one pointed at him and made a gesture
across his throat.

'Shhh!' said Marinetta, pulling at his
sleeve. 'You are too noisy.'

Lucius sat down again. 'I want to do
something,' he raged. 'They have violated
your home, and left my uncle for dead.'

'What would Titus have wished you to
do?' asked Marinetta.

Lucius thought for a long moment. He
knew that his uncle regarded him as being
headstrong, and always in the past it was
Uncle Titus, as his guardian, who had been

there to prevent him rushing in hastily. But now he wasn't with him. Lucius was on his own – well, not quite. He looked again at Marinetta.

'Let us talk this over slowly,' she said. 'If we declare ourselves to be Roman citizens, then we are of no value to them as slaves, and they will surely kill us. Also, your uncle is a government intelligence officer, isn't he?' she said shrewdly. 'So the name Calvus may not help us at the moment. We must choose our time very carefully to speak out.' She touched the folds of her dress. 'Remember I still have the message. What would be the best thing to do?'

'To remain quiet,' said Lucius reluctantly, 'and look for a way to escape. If we can. And then ... and then,' he went on, his voice rising higher in excitement, 'try to take the message ourselves to Stilicho in Rome!'

'Shhh,' said Marinetta again. She glanced around her. 'Where in Rome, exactly?'

'His home is by the army barracks, the Villa Viridis, in Via Tabula,' replied Lucius.

'If we are going across the sea to Gaul, then that takes us nearer to Rome, doesn't it?'

Lucius frowned as he remembered how long it had taken, marching with the legions, to travel up from Rome, through the Alps across Gaul, to the Mare Brittanicus. And then across that narrow channel to Britain. 'It is still many days' travel,' he said. 'And there is no way of knowing where this boat will dock.'

'We have no choice,' said Marinetta practically. 'But at least now we have a plan.'

She stopped speaking as a shrill bird call pierced the air. The two men jumped to their feet and pointed to where a boat had appeared offshore. Marinetta and Lucius were lifted up, carried through the shallows and heaved aboard. They heard the sound of conversation in a strange language and the chink of coins. In a few moments the pirates had turned the boat around and were making sail. The wind caught at once, and soon the little craft was heading out to sea.

Marinetta felt a terrible dread upon her. What awaited her beyond her own island? She turned her head and saw the long line of the coast becoming more distant. The far hills darkening as the boat sailed steadily on, further and further away from her friends and all that was familiar and loved. She slumped down among the coiled ropes beside the mast. She might never see her father, Lavinia, or her homeland again.

Lucius had also realised that they were being taken away by slave traders. That his life didn't mean anything to these brigands. Any hope of help from the Roman Army in Britain was now gone. Galleys patrolled the sea, but he knew that the Romans, unused to the tides and currents of these waters, would be no match for these pirates. He felt despondency creep up on him.

Beside him, Marinetta laid her head in her arms and wept.

Lucius cleared his throat. 'My deepest sorrow at your grief,' he said and held out his hand.

Marinetta looked at him. She knew the effort it must have cost him to offer his hand to her, a girl, and a Briton of Celtic origin. She reached out her hand and took his.

'Marinetta,' he said, using her name for the first time, 'we will find a way to escape.'

He pulled her gently to her feet and they watched the shores of Britain slip away. 'I promise you. We will find a way, together.'

8

Separated

So, thought Marinetta, this is what it is like to be a slave; made to do every menial task and given only broken bread for food. They were tied to the main mast by a long piece of thick rope, which gave them just enough movement to work, eat, and perform their toilet. At night their hands were also tied which meant that there was no chance of escape.

Marinetta began to notice each evening that, as darkness fell, Lucius would gaze intently at the heavens above them. 'Why do you look so carefully at the stars?' she asked him.

'No reason,' he said briefly, and he smiled at her. But she saw that he was frowning.

'There is a reason,' she insisted.

'Oh,' he said carelessly, 'I was thinking that … that … our paths crossing in such a manner… Perhaps it was written in the stars. After all, our lives were so very different, it is strange that we should meet.'

'Yes,' she agreed. 'I suppose it *is* strange. But perhaps we aren't so very different. We have both been brought up by men who hold responsible office, and we have had a great deal of freedom.'

'Not so much freedom now,' said Lucius bitterly.

'Well,' said Marinetta quickly, 'tell me about your upbringing, and your family.'

'My parents died when I was an infant,' said Lucius, 'and I have but one sister. She and her husband have a little shop in the Via Notte, near the Colosseum in Rome. They sell cotton and linen, and mix herbs and oils to dye them pretty colours. She painted the shop sign herself, beautiful purple and pink anemones on a dark green board.'

'You are very fond of your sister,' observed Marinetta.

'It is two years since I have seen her. When she and her husband married, my father's elder brother made me his ward. I have been his attendant as he travels about on army business.'

'And you enjoy it?' she asked him. 'Always being on the move, without a proper home?'

'Yes,' said Lucius. 'I like an army life. I am going to be a soldier.' He looked around him. '*Was* going to be a soldier,' he added, with sadness in his voice.

Marinetta laid her hand on his arm and they were silent for a while. Then his eyes were drawn back to the night sky and she saw the frown appear on his face again.

'Why do you stare at the stars?' she asked him again. 'You yourself said that our lives have become linked, so you *must* tell me.'

Lucius sighed and then turned to her. 'I don't have much knowledge of these matters...' He hesitated. 'But I think, by the position of the constellations, we are not sailing towards Gaul.'

'Where *are* we sailing then?' whispered Marinetta.

'Perhaps some port known to thieves and

pirates. I am not sure...' he hesitated.

'Tell me,' said Marinetta.

'Lusitania... Spain... Africa perhaps.'

And it was on the coast of Africa that they finally landed and were led down the gangplank to be sold in the harbour slave market.

'That one!' a rough voice from a neighbouring vessel called out at once. 'I'll take that boy there! One of my galley slaves has just died, and I must sail with the tide. How much?'

Within a few moments the master of the African galley had bargained with their captors and Lucius was dragged away struggling.

Marinetta was stunned. 'No!' she shrieked. 'No! Lucius!'

'Marinetta!' She heard him call. 'Be brave! I will find you!'

'Lucius!' she screamed again.

'Quiet!' One of the pirates struck her. 'Be quiet at once. You won't fetch a good price if people hear you screaming.'

'Then I shall scream loud and long,' she replied immediately.

He hit her again, harder. 'You might find yourself with an evil master then,' he told her. 'The more they pay, the better they treat their slaves. Keep a silent tongue!'

Marinetta stood, tears running down her face. Everyone knew that galley slaves, chained to their oars, were worked until they died. 'Lucius,' she sobbed. 'Lucius!'

'Don't cry, little one,' someone spoke beside her. 'I am buying for the great family of Gaius Dalius. I think I shall take you.'

Marinetta turned and looked with revulsion at the small fat man who stood beside her.

'Go away,' she said. 'I don't want to be bought.'

'Come now,' he coaxed her. 'They are travelling back to Rome tomorrow, and my mistress Aemilia wants a new maid to attend to her comforts. And,' he reached out his hand to touch Marinetta's head, 'that beautiful hair will make her a fine new wig. None of her friends will have one that colour.'

Marinetta shrank back as the little man stroked her hair.

'Like the sun,' he said. 'A golden sun.'

'The girl with the golden hair!' a new, louder voice shouted out across the market place. And someone pushed their way through the throng.

'Salmanes,' cried Marinetta. 'Salmanes!' And she began to cry even more.

'I heard you were captured by brigands,' said the trader. 'Titus Calvus found his way back to a fort on the Wall, where, luckily, the soldiers are loyal to Rome.'

'So he is safe,' Marinetta said. 'And my father?'

'He and Lavinia are well, but grieving for you. He has sent messages to the Celtic tribes with promises of gold and silver for your safe return.' The trader smiled a huge grin. 'And I have found you! I will buy you at once.' He turned to the brigand who was holding the rope around Marinetta's wrist. 'A fair price for the girl?'

But the pirate had overheard their conversation. 'A thousand sestertii,' he said with a cunning smile.

Salmanes gasped. 'A thousand! I do not have that amount.'

'Find it,' came the reply.

Marinetta looked at Salmanes desperately, her eyes filling up with tears. He pulled at his beard. 'Even if I sold all my goods...'

'Make up your mind,' said the pirate, 'otherwise she goes to the first buyer. We don't want to miss the tide.'

'The tide,' thought Marinetta. 'The tide!' she cried aloud. 'Lucius!'

'Lucius?' repeated Salmanes.

'Yes,' said Marinetta, 'he was here with me, and has just been sold to the owner of that African galley. They leave with the tide.' Quickly she dried her eyes and rubbed her hands across her face. 'Salmanes,' she spoke firmly, 'you must keep all your money and go at once to the harbour and buy Lucius.' She took the rolled parchment from inside her dress and slipped it secretly into Salmanes' hands. 'Give him this. Buy him rather than me now, or he will be lost forever. Go!' Her voice was stronger now. 'I beg you.' She looked around to where the fat man was standing. 'That house slave will buy me to travel with his mistress to Rome. Tell Lucius this. Ask him to look for me there at the house of Gaius Dalius, after he does what we agreed.'

'Please,' she urged as Salmanes hesitated. 'It is the most sensible plan. Lucius is in the greatest danger.' She lowered her voice. 'Once I am in Rome I can go to the authorities and declare my citizenship in safety.'

'You are lucky,' the house slave informed her, as he led her away, 'to belong to such a rich and powerful family. Soon you will be in the most magnificent city in all the world – Rome.'

9

Journey to Rome

They cut off Marinetta's hair that very night. Leah, a tall Nubian slave woman, tied back the golden curls, and with a great pair of shears sliced through the hair at the nape of Marinetta's neck. She held up the long mane. 'It shines like a golden fire,' she said.

Marinetta looked at it and burst into tears.

'Hush now,' said the older woman. She sat down and put her arm around the distraught girl. 'When the mistress Aemilia sees this she will be so happy. On the return journey to Rome tomorrow you will have the least to do.'

As Leah had predicted, Marinetta was left alone for much of the time the next day as the galley made its way around the African coast, and then sailed on towards Italy. She watched the others running errands, or standing for hours fanning their owners with huge peacock fans. Aemilia seemed placid and undemanding, but there was something cold and arrogant about Gaius Dalius which made Marinetta nervous.

'What business had he in such a place as we have just left?' Marinetta asked Leah. 'They have no goods on board for trade. Where does their great wealth come from?'

'Better not to ask, little one,' came the whispered reply. 'I will tell you only this. If you want someone to disappear and have enough gold...'

Marinetta shivered. She was glad now that she hadn't told anyone the story of what had happened to her and Lucius. It had been treachery in Britain which had caused the attack on her father's house and them to be sold as slaves. Better to remain silent until she found out who she could trust in Rome. 'You mean he kills people for payment?' she asked Leah. 'Surely the authorities will seek him out and punish him?'

Leah laughed. 'Far from it,' she said.

'Consuls and kings come knocking on his door. It is a very lucrative trade.' She glanced around. 'Talk such as this is dangerous ... let us speak no more.'

They disembarked in Italy, at Ostia. From the ship Marinetta could see the lighthouse in the harbour and the bustling docks. She gasped as an enormous grey monstrous creature with an elongated nose lumbered along the pier. Long chains dragged behind it as it pulled a large pile of logs towards the dockside.

'What is it?'

Leah smiled at her. 'It is called an elephant,' she said. 'They are very gentle, despite their size.'

The animal raised its trunk and made a loud trumpeting sound. Marinetta shrank back in terror. 'I don't believe you,' she said.

The women slaves were to travel with their master and mistress by riverboat and Marinetta saw her first sight of the eternal city as they sailed up the River Tiber. The gleaming white columns, triumphal arches, wide paved streets, and so many people! The barge finally set them down next to a path which led directly to the spacious villa belonging to Gaius Dalius.

Some of Marinetta's duties were in the kitchen, and she very quickly learned to obey orders speedily. A frown or an angry glance from the master sent Radulphus the head slave scurrying off in fear, and then he boxed the ears of anyone within reach. Marinetta tried not to dwell on the fact that now her welfare, perhaps even her life, depended on the whim of others.

On this first night in Rome, Gaius Dalius was expecting a guest for dinner, and Radulphus had already cuffed the kitchen boy twice about the head.

'The meal must be perfect,' he shouted. 'Tonight we entertain a very important person.'

Marinetta had been sweeping the yard when the visitor arrived, a tall man with grey hair and hard blue eyes.

The main course was sent back twice. First it wasn't warm enough, then it was too hot. Marinetta heard the angry voice of Gaius Dalius shouting orders at the head slave.

'See to it in person, this time!' And as his

66

slave went to hurry away, he called. 'Have more wine brought... at once!'

'You girl!' Radulphus snatched the broom from Marinetta's hand. 'Take the wine jug to the dining room. *Now!*' he yelled as she hesitated.

Marinetta lifted the pitcher of wine and carried it carefully to the dining room. The mistress had retired early and the men were lolling on their couches chatting. They did not stop talking as they held up their goblets. Marinetta moved discreetly. She had been told that a slave should not be noticed, had to be invisible. And was of such little account, that the two Romans did not dream that the young British girl who poured their wine would understand their language.

'So you will do this service for me?' It was the visitor who spoke.

'The matter will be seen to at once,' replied Gaius Dalius. 'If this secret message tells the commander of the army the names of officers in Britain who are ready to revolt, and links them to our senator friend, then it *must* be intercepted.' His mouth twisted in a cruel smile. 'And, lest he should speak of it to others, I will arrange a special welcome outside Stilicho's villa for the messenger himself.'

'It must be done soon,' said the other man. 'My spies tell me he is riding hard towards Rome at this very moment.'

Gaius Dalius drank deeply and held out his silver wine cup for Marinetta to fill once more. 'I will call my men and arrange it now,' he said. 'Do we know the name of this messenger?'

Marinetta tilted the jug to pour the wine.

'Yes,' replied her master's dinner guest. 'He is called Lucius Calvus.'

10

Assassins in Rome

'Clumsy fool!'

Gaius Dalius slapped Marinetta's arm as she stared stupidly at the wine dribbling across the table.

Lucius! The man with the grey hair had just said his name! Marinetta's hand remained motionless for a second, and then she mumbled an apology and hurried off to find a cloth. Her fingers were shaking as she returned and quickly sponged the droplets away.

'Lucius!' she whispered as she ran back to the kitchens. His name was in her head, the thought of him filling her whole mind. Lucius! He was here! He must have escaped, or Salmanes had managed to buy him and give him his freedom. And, by what she had overheard, he was not very far from Rome. Soon he would be making his way to Stilicho's villa, and into a trap!

What should she do? She had to warn him. Somehow she had to make her way through the streets of Rome, find him, and warn him. But where in the city could he be? Marinetta thought desperately. Where? Where would he go? Her whole body trembled as she tried to think clearly. Of course! To his family – to the house of his sister! And where was that? What had he told her on their journey from Britain? Yes, now she remembered Lucius telling her the name of the street, the Via Notte, not far from the Colosseum, and the description of the shop sign. Purple flowers painted on green board. She *must* find it.

Marinetta spoke pleadingly to Radulphus. 'I feel unwell,' she told him. 'Might I be allowed to retire?'

He stared at her suspiciously. 'Unwell when there is work to be done,' he said. Then he peered at her more closely. 'Your face is quite flushed, and you are shaking, child. Go and rest. If you have a fever, then you are best away from the rest of us.'

Marinetta thanked him and left. But instead of climbing the stairs to her little room, she picked up a long scarf to cover her head, and, slipping quietly out of a side door, she ran to the gate in the wall.

She had gone no more than a few paces from the end of the street when she realised that she had no idea which way to turn.

It was getting darker as Marinetta walked towards what seemed to be the main road. There were rough men about, men who had been drinking and were ready to argue with anyone. She must avoid trouble. If she were found and returned to her household, the punishment would be terrible. As a runaway slave she could be branded, or have one of her hands cut off. Marinetta shivered. A group of youths went past laughing, and she stepped quickly into a doorway.

'Little sister,' one of them stopped and looked at her. 'Why are you abroad at this time of night?'

Marinetta thought fast. 'My mother is ill,'

she said. 'I have been sent to fetch the physician. He stays in the Via Notte, near the Colosseum.' She looked imploringly at the young man. 'I fear I have lost my way.'

'No, no,' the youth said. 'Look, you are very near. I'll show you.' As he took Marinetta's arm and led her across the street his friends began to whistle. He shouted back and waved at them.

Marinetta's breath came in short gasps. His hold on her arm was very firm. They were approaching the corner where a blazing brazier stood to light the way. Although she didn't have a slave's collar around her neck, he might be able to guess by her clothes that she was not a free woman.

'Ah,' she said, as they came nearer to the junction. 'I see where I am now. Thank you, sir, and good night.'

The boy smiled and let her arm go reluctantly.

'My mother...' said Marinetta. 'I must hurry.' And she walked away from him.

'The other way, little sister,' he said.

Marinetta turned immediately. 'Of course,' she said, and nodded.

'Then take the left fork,' he called after her.

Marinetta raised her arm in salute and kept walking. She heard him laugh and then run off.

She almost missed it. The dark greens and purples of the painted flowers on the sign merged with the blackness of the night. It was only the soft creaking noise which she heard above her head, that made her glance upwards.

'Ah,' she gasped aloud and her heart quickened. She stepped up to the door and battered on it with both fists. Eventually a shutter at a first-floor window was flung open.

'Hush,' ordered a woman's cross voice, 'you will wake my baby!'

'Let me in!' cried Marinetta. 'I am a friend of Lucius Calvus. He told me this was the house of his sister Serena.'

'I am Serena,' said the woman. 'Wait please.'

In a few moments Serena had unbarred the door and Marinetta was inside babbling out her story.

Serena gasped, and put her hand to her mouth. 'Lucius did not tell me all of this. He was here half an hour since, changed his clothes, and then said he had come on urgent business to see the commander-in-chief of the army at his villa. My husband is away buying goods for our shop. I would never have let Lucius go if I had realised.'

Marinetta was thinking even as Serena was speaking. 'I must follow him and try to warn him.'

'I cannot leave my baby,' said Serena. 'And anyway...' She pointed to the burning candle marked with the hours which stood on her table. 'You will be too late.'

The two women stared at each other.

'I *must* try,' said Marinetta.

Serena nodded. She went to open the outside door, and stopped. 'I will draw you a map, and ... your hair is shorn. I can give you clothes to dress as a boy. You will be safer like that.'

Five minutes later a slim boyish figure was running fast in the direction of Stilicho's villa.

It wasn't until she had reached the Villa Viridis that Marinetta stopped to think about how she would actually get in to see Stilicho. Staying in the darkness, she walked all around the perimeter walls. She counted two gates in the high walls, both well guarded. From within the courtyards she could hear dogs barking.

It's impossible, thought Marinetta. Stilicho's guards would never let her past the gate. Perhaps she could find another way in...

Then she noticed that there was a line of trees growing close to the villa. Although their branches did not quite reach to the wall, perhaps if she climbed out along one of them she could swing herself across from the branch on to the top of the wall?

She quietly crept in the shadows until she stood under the tree which grew closest to the wall. Her heart was beating fast, and she leaned for a moment against its broad trunk. The branches above her stirred softly and then a figure dropped silently to the ground behind her. Marinetta heard a noise and half turned, but too late. Two hands gripped her roughly round the neck and began to squeeze her throat.

11

Commander Stilicho

Marinetta put her hands up to her neck and tried to prise away the hard fingers which were choking her, but they only held her more tightly. She could not speak or cry out, so intense was the pressure. Her ears were thrumming, her eyes watered and she realised that she was losing consciousness. She raised her hands in one last effort. As she tried to free herself she half twisted round, and saw her attacker.

And he saw her.

'Marinetta!' cried Lucius. He released his hold and she fell to the ground. 'Marinetta!' he said again. 'What are you doing here?'

'Looking for you,' she gasped. 'I overheard talk in my master's house tonight.' She coughed, and drew breath again. 'Assassins have been sent to intercept you.' She took his arm and struggled to her feet. 'Your name was known to them, Lucius. They had found out that you carried a most important message.'

Lucius helped her to lean against the tree. He touched her head. 'Your hair,' he said. 'Your beautiful hair.'

Marinetta took her hand away. 'Don't speak of that just now. Your life is threatened. Someone brought word of your mission, although I don't know how he learned of it.'

'I think I might know,' said Lucius wretchedly. 'After your merchant friend paid for my release, I boasted of being an emissary of Rome.' He struck his forehead with his hand. 'I, who have been told often enough by my uncle to guard my tongue, could not be quiet! I had to tell everyone I met how important I was.' He looked down at the slight girl standing beside him. 'You, who have risked your life to help me... I must tell you, Marinetta, that I am not worthy of it.'

Marinetta surveyed him for a moment. 'Most like you are not,' she said crisply. 'But, as we have come this far, let us now make sure the message reaches the commander-in-chief, lest your uncle be disappointed.'

Unfortunately, I fear he *will* be disappointed,' said a voice behind them. 'I must ask you to give me the message that you carry.'

Marinetta and Lucius turned to find themselves surrounded by three men, each carrying knives. Lucius reached for his own knife.

'Don't be foolish, boy,' said one of the assassins. 'There are three of us and one of you.'

Lucius hesitated.

'Two of us, in fact,' said Marinetta. She moved as she spoke, bringing her knee up into the groin of the man directly in front of her. Then she ran ... straight for the main gate of the villa further along the wall, screaming loudly as she went, 'Help! I am being attacked! Help! Defend me, an innocent girl! Help! Help!'

She heard footsteps beside her and saw that it was Lucius, and was glad that for once he had chosen flight over foolhardy braveness.

Stilicho's guards reacted quickly, racing across the street, spears held out in front of them. The assassins scattered into the shadows.

Once they were both in the guard house, Lucius identified himself to the chief guard and asked to speak to the commander-in-chief of the army.

The guard laughed. 'It is only big fish the commander sees, not tiddlers like you.'

Lucius stood directly in front of the man, arms folded across his chest. 'Listen carefully to me,' he declared haughtily. 'We have travelled from Britain, for many weeks and in great danger, to deliver a message from my uncle. His name is Titus Calvus, a senior officer of the emperor, Flavius Honorius.' He glared at the man before him. 'Bring me to the commander at once! You delay us on peril of your life.'

The man eyed Lucius warily. He was used to taking orders and this pup obviously knew how to give them out, young though

79

he was. And the Emperor himself was only a callow youth, who had inherited on his father's death when only ten years old. Also, the name Titus Calvus was known to him. A man whom the senior army officials consulted when campaigns were being planned. Better be careful ... his pension could be lost by a moment's stupidity.

He led them through the courtyard and into a large room where maps covered the walls.

'Wait here,' he said.

They waited for over an hour, and as they did, Marinetta and Lucius talked quietly of how they had both journeyed to Rome. Salmanes had bargained with the galley master and then secured Lucius a passage on a fishing vessel going to Naples.

'How can we repay him?' said Marinetta.

Lucius laughed. 'He said he will make a special trip to Britain to collect his reward.'

And then Marinetta told Lucius her story. When she described how her hair had been cut off, Lucius raised his hand and touched her head. 'It will grow again,' he said gently.

Suddenly they heard the sound of

marching feet. The curtain at the end of the room was swept aside and the chief guard appeared. 'Flavius Stilicho, the commander-in-chief!' he announced.

A tall figure strode into the room, his toga edged in purple and gold. He looked at Marinetta and Lucius with clear sharp eyes. 'You bring me news from Britain? A message from Titus Calvus?'

Lucius leapt to his feet. He brought his arm across his chest in salute.

Stilicho listened carefully as Lucius spoke and then took the precious piece of bark and read the message. He sighed heavily. 'It is as we suspected. At any sign of trouble the jackals creep out. The Emperor will decide the fate of the disloyal senator named here, and also Gaius Dalius and his assassins. By now my friend Titus and the garrison commander Cornelius will have dealt with the traitors in Britain.' He smiled at them. 'You will be well rewarded for your efforts on behalf of Rome. I'll arrange safe conduct home for you both.'

'And you will send troops to reinforce the Wall?' asked Lucius.

'For the moment I will send men to accompany you on your journey and also some supplies. That should help a little…'

'But we need more!' cried Marinetta before she could help herself.

Stilicho turned his hard gaze on her.

'Your pardon, sir,' said Lucius, quickly stepping forward.

Stilicho raised his hand. 'I understand how you must feel. You have travelled so far, and so bravely, to bring me this message, and tell me of the local situation. But look now,' he spoke more gently, 'let me show you on the map where our enemies press closely upon us on all sides.'

Marinetta and Lucius gazed at the huge map of the known world which hung on one wall. It showed the Eastern Empire, Syria, Egypt, Africa. Mountain ranges, rivers, seas and lakes. And then the Western Empire – Gaul, Lusitania, Hispania, Hibernia.

The world was so vast, thought Marinetta. And then she saw Britain. A little island tacked on at the top. 'How tiny we are,' she spoke aloud without realising it.

'But not unimportant,' said Stilicho kindly.

'Are you saying we will have to fend for ourselves?' asked Lucius.

Marinetta glanced sideways at Lucius's face. He had said 'we'.

'Go home to Britain,' said Stilicho. 'Protect your homes and keep them safe until I can send more troops. I believe that you will find the strength and resources to do this. And soon, I promise you, I will give orders for a relief force.' He grasped both of their hands in his own. 'You will win through ... because you do it, not for conquest, nor for duty, but for the love that you bear your homeland.'

12

Home to Britain

The early morning mist which had begun as a thin line on the horizon, had crept up on the boat as the sun rose, and was now seeping around the two figures standing together in the prow.

So different from the haze which shimmered at sunrise over the blue waters of the Mediterranean Sea, thought Marinetta. She pulled the soft woollen cloak which Lucius's sister had given her more closely around her shoulders. Beside her, Lucius coughed.

'Cursed British weather,' he grumbled. 'Such a welcome home for you.'

'I don't care,' said Marinetta happily. She strained her eyes to see through the fine sea fog, eager to catch a glimpse of the shoreline.

The tide was running against them and the oarsmen were having to pull hard to keep their craft on course. They were still far from the coast of northern Britain but Marinetta had been awake since dawn. At first light she had taken up her position at the front of the boat. Five long weeks it had taken them to get a safe passage on an official supply ship, and make the journey back to Britain. They had sent word to their families to tell them that they were well and travelling home.

Marinetta shivered and Lucius took his own cloak and placed it around her shoulders for extra warmth. Marinetta noticed that he did not take his hands away. And she could not stop herself from grasping hold of his arm, in her turn, when she saw through the shifting fog the suddenly looming headland which was her first sight of Britain.

A wide sweep of bay surrounded the rocky outcrop. There was a shingle beach, and, stretching back from the water's edge, long meadows and dark evergreen trees. What a difference from the ochre-tiled roofs and the red earth of the countryside around Rome.

'Oh,' said Marinetta. She put her hand to her eyes as she felt them fill with tears. 'I had forgotten how green and beautiful my own country is.'

Lucius gripped her shoulders. 'Yes,' he agreed, 'the rain makes the woods and fields gentle and deep.'

They moved closer to the land as the boat turned to sail up the broad estuary which would take them to the fort at Maia. From there they would travel eastwards along the Wall, then home to Corstopitum.

'Will your uncle be at the garrison?' Marinetta asked Lucius.

Lucius nodded his head. 'Unless some other unrest has suddenly called him away. I told him as much as I felt it was wise to write down in a letter. I am sure he will have guessed the rest.'

Marinetta looked up at him. 'What do you think will happen, eventually, in Britain?'

'Who knows?' said Lucius. 'If the soldiers are unpaid they will drift away. They may be ordered back to fight in the Eastern Empire, and they might resent this and choose to rebel. If they find a strong leader...' he laughed dryly. 'We could find ourselves with a new Emperor.'

Marinetta shivered. 'My father says the law protects all,' said Marinetta. 'If there is no order, then destruction follows.'

'Perhaps we should choose somewhere else to live?'

Marinetta looked at Lucius. He had said 'we' again, and she realised that she thought in the same way. That their lives were now linked, their fates and future intertwined.

'But where would we go?' she asked him. 'What place is safe? And anyway, my father will not leave his home. Also...' she continued slowly, 'all the more reason for us to return to Britain at this time. Someone must try to keep a lamp burning if there is a dark night ahead.'

'Fine words, Marinetta,' said Lucius.

She looked at him closely and saw that he was not teasing her.

'What will you do?' she asked him. 'Will you still make your life in the army?'

'Perhaps not,' said Lucius. 'I think I might take training in law.' He grinned at her. 'Your father may need an assistant, and then you and I can both help him to keep this civilisation of ours from crumbling away.'

They had proceeded so far upriver that they could now see the outline of the fort at Maia which guarded the gateway to the sea.

'Some things which the Romans brought are so obviously good that they will never be lost,' said Marinetta. She raised her arm and pointed at the fort. 'There is proof of what we have and what we are. And beyond that lies Hadrian's Wall. It will last for a thousand years or more.'

Glossary

Alms   Money or goods given to people in need, as charity.

Aqueduct   A channel made of brick or stone designed to bring clean water to a town.

Brand   A burning piece of wood used as a torch.

Brazier   A portable grill holding a charcoal or wood fire.

Brigand   A bandit or plunderer, usually found in wild or isolated areas.

Caledonia   Roman name for the northern part of Britain.

Celts   A group of people with their own language who lived in Britain, Gaul, Spain and other parts of Western Europe in pre-Roman times.

Colosseum   A large amphitheatre in Rome, where sports and other public entertainment took place.

Consul   A chief magistrate who governed ancient Rome. Each year two people were elected to this position, which gave them the highest authority in the Roman republic.

Emissary An agent or representative sent on a particular mission, often by the government or head of state.

Fresco A painting done on a plaster wall or ceiling.

Galley A type of boat.

Garrison A military fort where troops are stationed.

Gaul An area covering ancient France and Belgium, and also parts of Italy, the Netherlands and Germany.

Glacis slope A defensive slope in front of a fortification designed to make it easier to fire on attacking forces.

Hadrian's Wall A fortified wall built across northern England, on the orders of Roman emperor Hadrian, as a defence against the northern British tribes.

Hibernia Roman name for Ireland.

Hispania Roman name for Spain and Portugal.

Manoeuvres Large-scale military training exercises.

Mosaic   Picture or design made with small pieces of coloured material, such as glass or tile, stuck onto a surface.

Nubians   People from Nubia, a region in north-east Africa.

Picts   Members of an ancient people living in the north of Scotland.

Renegade   An outlaw or rebel.

Saxons   West Germanic people, who later settled in parts of southern Britain in the 5th and 6th centuries.

Senator   A member of the senate, the legislative council of ancient Rome.

Sentry   A soldier who keeps watch and guards a place.

Thessaly   A region in Greece.

Toga   A wool robe worn wrapped around the body by Roman men and women.

Vandal   A member of a Germanic people that raided the Roman provinces.

Via   Latin word for way or road.

Historical Note

The territory controlled by ancient Rome stretched from north-western Europe to the Near East, and covered all the lands of the Mediterranean and parts of north Africa. Britain was the northernmost point of this huge Empire, which sometimes made it difficult for Rome to control.

When the Romans decided to add a new territory to their Empire they needed to consider two factors. Did they have enough troops and would the riches to be gained through conquest cover the cost of an invasion? The Roman General Julius Caesar made the first attempt of invasion in 55 BC, following his conquest of France. The conquest of Britain would bring further prestige and it was known that there was gold and silver to be found there.

At that time, the Celts ruled Britain. They were divided into different tribes, each led by chiefs. Neighbouring tribes would often quarrel and this sometimes led to vicious battles in which fierce warriors would ride out in chariots to attack each other. So although there was no unified army to face the Roman troops, the Celts were well practised in the arts of war and Julius Caesar was defeated. He attempted another invasion the following year, but this had to be abandoned when his troops were needed back in France.

The Romans weren't successful until nearly 100 years later in AD 43. Claudius had recently become Emperor and wanted to secure his position by expanding his empire to the British Isles. This time the Roman Army succeeded in capturing the land of the Catuvellauni tribe and its capital Camulodunum (Colchester). This became the first capital of the new Roman province of Britannia. But the British did not give in that easily. Other Celtic chiefs, particularly in Wales and the north, continued to fight, although their opposition posed no real threat to the well-organised Roman forces. By around AD 80 Wales and the north of England were under Roman rule.

The Romans pushed gradually north,

driven by the need to secure their frontiers and the desire of their leaders to win prestige, but Scotland proved more tricky and the territory was often lost almost as soon as it was gained. In AD 122 Emperor Hadrian decided that it was a lost cause – rather than conquering the Scottish tribes, he'd settle for keeping them at bay. He ordered for a wall to be built right across the country to divide Roman Britain from Scotland and 'separate Romans from Barbarians'.

The stone wall was a monument to the power of the Roman Empire and was its greatest single engineering project. It took six years to build and ran 73 miles, from Solway Firth in the west to the River Tyne in the east. Every Roman mile there was a gateway guarded by a small fort, known as a milecastle. You can still walk along parts of the wall today.

Twenty years later, in AD 140, Hadrian's successor, Antonius Pius built a second wall farther north into Scotland. This was called the Antonine Wall. However, unlike Hadrian's Wall, this was only built in turf fronted by a ditch, and did not last long. In AD 181 the northern tribes poured over the wall and pushed the Romans back to Hadrian's Wall. From then on, for nearly 300 years, Hadrian's Wall marked the furthermost limit of the Roman Empire.

The Romans brought stability, unity and wealth to Britain for nearly four centuries. However, by the end of the second century Rome was in decline and Roman troops were gradually pulled out of Britain to deal with emergencies elsewhere in the Empire. In AD 410 the Britons sent a petition to the Emperor Honorious asking for help against invaders. He replied that from now on they must 'see to there own defences'. In the end, the Romans were not driven out by the British; Britain was simply abandoned.

Map of Roman Britain

CALEDONIA
(Scotland)

ANTONINE WALL

HADRIAN'S WALL

CORSTOPITUM
(Corbridge)

EBURACUM
(York)

LINDUM
(Lincoln)

HIBERNIA
(Ireland)

BRITANNIA

CAMULODUNUM
(Colchester)

GLEVUM
(Gloucester)

VERULAMIUM
(St Albans)

LONDINIUM
(London)